GW00372139

CLOSE ENCOUNTERS

Close Encounters is the first book by Donovan which is the pseudonym adopted by Rupert Fawcett for his new series of cartoons. Rupert is also the creator of the highly successful Fred cartoon series. He lives in West London with his wife and baby son.

Close Encounters greeting cards are available throughout the world, published by Blackwood Publishing, 22 Bridge Street, Walton-on-Thames, Surrey, KT12 1AQ.

Also by Rupert Fawcett

Fred
More Fred
The Extraordinary World of Fred

CLOSE ENCOUNTERS

by

HEADLINE

Published in association with
Blackwood Publishing

Copyright © 1993 Rupert Fawcett

The right of Rupert Fawcett to be identified as the author of
the work has been asserted by him in accordance with the
Copyright, Designs and Patents Act 1988.

First published in 1993
by HEADLINE BOOK PUBLISHING PLC
Published in association with Blackwood Publishing

10 9 8 7 6 5 4 3 2 1

British Library Cataloguing in Publication Data

Donovan
Close Encounters
I. Title
741.5

ISBN 0-7472-0922-7 (hardback)

ISBN 0 7472 7875 X (softback)

Printed and bound in Great Britain by
BPCC Hazell Books Ltd
Member of BPCC Ltd

HEADLINE BOOK BUBLISHING PLC
Headline House
79 Great Titchfield Street
London W1P 7FN

PERCH — TALK

AUDREY SENSED THAT ALAN
WAS SOMEHOW DIFFERENT FROM
ALL THE OTHER GUYS

'O.K., SO YOU DON'T LIKE RED HAIR, BIG NOSES OR LARGE FEET. NOW, WHAT **DO** YOU LIKE IN A MAN?'

'I'LL FIND THAT 'G' SPOT IF IT'S
THE LAST THING I DO',
STORMED STEPHEN

MRS GINSBERG'S GUESTS ALWAYS
FOUND HER A MOST THOUGHTFUL
AND ATTENTIVE HOSTESS

IT WAS THE HEAVY MOB FROM
DEAD MAN'S CREEK, BONECRUSHER
BILL, IRONFIST FRANK AND
EMBARRASSING ED

GORDON HAD THE UNPLEASANT
FEELING THAT HE HAD MISJUDGED
THE SITUATION

AFTER MUCH PERSUASION THERESA
FINALLY GAVE TERENCE PERMISSION
TO ADJUST HER HORIZONTAL HOLD

LITTLE CREEK HAD BECOME A
MUCH SAFER PLACE SINCE ALL
THE GUNS WERE CONFISCATED

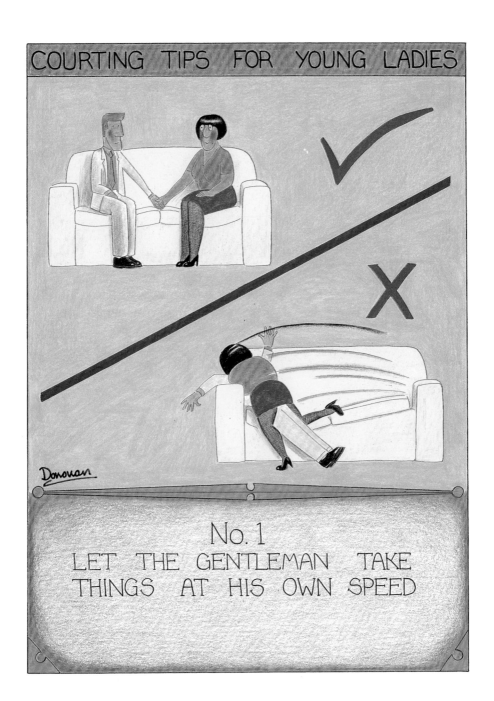

BABS WASN'T GOING TO
LET THIS ONE GET AWAY

DESMOND'S LIFE WAS ALWAYS SO
FULL OF DRAMA

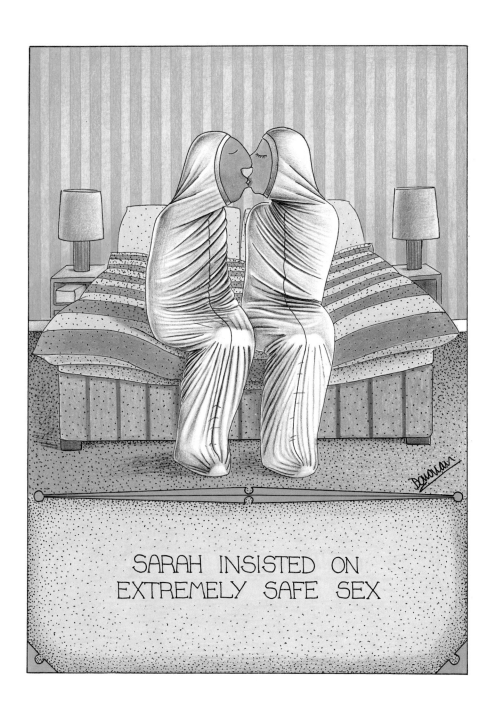

SARAH INSISTED ON
EXTREMELY SAFE SEX

GEORGE HAD BEEN TOLD
ABOUT THE SEDUCTIVE
POWER OF HUMOUR

SITTING BULL AND PASSING CLOUD LISTENED
PATIENTLY WHILE LITTLE THUNDER PROTESTED
ABOUT HAVING TO SHARE A WIG-WAM
WITH BREAKING WIND

CELIA CERTAINLY KNEW HOW TO
MAKE A CHAP FEEL SMALL

IT WAS THE MOMENT THE DOGGY-SUIT'S
PRINCIPAL DESIGN FAULT BECAME APPARENT

DORIS AND ALBERT WERE LIVING PROOF
THAT YOU ARE AS OLD AS YOU FEEL

PHILIP SUDDENLY FELT TERRIBLY
DULL AND PEDESTRIAN WITH
HIS SALTED CASHEWS

'I LIKE A WOMAN WHO KNOWS WHAT SHE WANTS IN LIFE AND IS PREPARED TO REACH OUT AND GRAB IT', BABBLED BASIL

HANK REALISED HE HAD ALWAYS
BEEN MILDLY IRRITATED BY CACTUS
BILL'S GAUDY NECKERCHIEFS

SIMON AND SARAH SPENT THEIR
FIRST DATE DISCUSSING OPERA,
MODERN ART AND FEMINISM
IN THE NINETIES

'YOU'RE JUST A GREAT BIG
BABY AREN'T YOU', COOED CLARISSA

JONATHAN SHAMEFULLY CONFESSED TO
GLORIA THAT HIS INTEREST IN HER
WAS PURELY PHYSICAL

LITTLE DID YOUNG ABDUL KNOW THAT
HE WAS TO PROVIDE THE INSPIRATION
FOR THE NOW FAMOUS OLD PROVERB,
'HALF A CAMEL IS BETTER THAN NO CAMEL'.

THE GREAT THING ABOUT PAUL AND PRUNELLA'S RELATIONSHIP WAS THAT THEY SHARED EXACTLY THE SAME TASTE

AFTER A COUPLE OF DRINKS BILL COULD SENSE
BARBARA BEGINNING TO RELAX

'SO THERE ISN'T INTELLIGENT LIFE ON MARS AFTER ALL', OBSERVED THE CAPTAIN

AT LAST ARTHUR WAS CAUGHT
IN THE ACT

EVERYBODY WAS GETTING INTO
THE CHRISTMAS SPIRIT

FOR PARANOID PETE SOME DAYS
WERE WORSE THAN OTHERS